D-BOT SQUAD

BOOK 3
Double Trouble

MAC PARK

Illustrated by JAMES HART

ALLEN&UNWIN
SYDNEY·MELBOURNE·AUCKLAND·LONDON

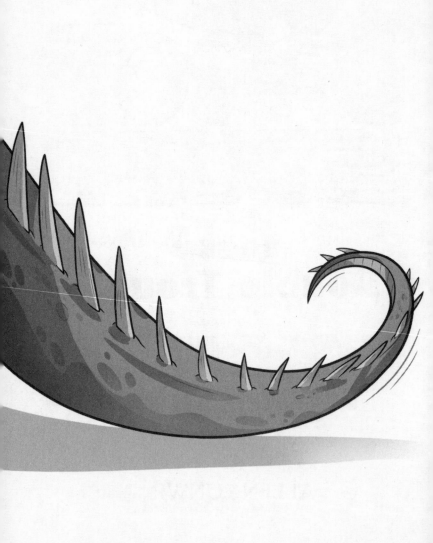

Chapter One

Hunter Marks was in big trouble. A huge flying dinosaur had him in its grip. Hunter was hanging from the dinosaur's claw. He was high in the sky.

Hunter stared at the claw gripping him around the middle. *If the dino lets go, I'll fall*, he thought. He grabbed the dinosaur's leg with both hands. Then he looked at his dino-bot. It was hanging from the dinosaur's other claw, swinging in the wind.

'Please don't drop my d-bot,'
Hunter said. 'I wish the remote
still worked. I wish my d-bot
could still fly. Then maybe I
could get myself out of this mess.'

The quetzelcoatlus flapped its
wings.

Flap! Flap! Flap!

It soared even higher.

Where is this dinosaur taking me?
Hunter thought. *Ms Stegg was
right – I did need help.*

Ms Stegg had sent Hunter out
to find a pterodactyl. And
Hunter had done his job. He'd
caught it and sent it back to
Dino Corp's secret dino-park.

After that, Hunter should have gone back to D-Bot Squad base. But he hadn't. He'd seen the bigger dino and thought he could catch it. **Alone.** But the bigger dino caught him instead.

The dino stopped flapping its wings and glided on the wind.

Gliding feels so smooth, Hunter thought. *It's like riding a flying fox at the park, only way better. A real quetzalcoatlus, gliding along in* **my** *world! Who would believe this?*

Hunter looked from one wing tip to the other.

'Your open wings are longer than a bus,' he said. 'Such huge wings on such a small body! The small body keeps you light. That's why you can fly so well.'

The dinosaur let out a very loud noise.

'Squaaarrk!'

Hunter thought his ears might burst. 'Uuuurgh!' he cried. Then he saw something else in the sky. 'Oh no, another flying dino! And it's coming this way.'

Why didn't I listen to Ms Stegg? thought Hunter. *She said this dinosaur was too strong for one person. And now there are* **two** *of them!*

Hunter knew he had to call Ms Stegg for help. That meant letting go of the dinosaur's leg to use his d-band.

Hunter moved his hands closer together. *Okay, I'll take one hand off the leg*, he thought. *I'll tap the 'talk' button on the d-band* **super-quickly**. *Then I'll hang on with both hands again. Easy, right?*

Hunter looked at the sea below, where some seagulls looked like tiny dots. His heart raced.

Hunter took a few deep breaths. He slowly opened one hand. But as he let go of the dino's leg, it opened its claw.

'**No!**' Hunter cried. '**Don't drop me!**'

Chapter Two

The dinosaur grabbed Hunter
again just in time. He let out a
big breath. 'That was close. I
need a new plan.' His mind
worked quickly.

Hunter moved one hand onto
the dinosaur's foot. He tried to
pull himself free from the claws.
But it was no good. The
dinosaur was too strong.

What can I do? thought Hunter.
*Now that I want it to let me go,
it won't!*

The dinosaur let out a huge cry.

'Squuuaaaark! Squuuaaaark!'

It had seen the other dinosaur flying towards it.

Hunter looked up. *That thing is really moving*, he thought. *I have to get on this dinosaur's back, fast!*

But there was nothing Hunter
could do. He watched, wide-
eyed, as the other dinosaur got
closer and closer.

What is it? Hunter thought. *It
has a long neck, but it's got wings.
And what's on the end of its tail?
It's not like any dinosaur I know.*

'Of course!' Hunter cried suddenly. 'It's a d-bot! It has to be.'

As the bot gained on them, Hunter could see its rider. 'It's carrying another D-Bot Squad member. Phew!'

A voice boomed through
Hunter's d-band speaker.

'I'm going to fly past you. Then
I'll turn around and come back
under you. Drop down onto my
d-bot's long neck when I say so.
Okay?'

*I hope she knows what she's
doing*, thought Hunter.

'Did you hear me?' the rider asked.

'I heard you,' Hunter said. 'But it's got me in its claws. I can't pull myself free. It's too strong.'

'Tickle its foot,' the rider said.

Is she for real? thought Hunter.

Hunter checked out the d-bot as it flew past him. It was built for super-fast flying. *It's like a rocket, only better*, Hunter thought. *It will be taller on the ground than this dinosaur, too. That's clever. I could build a better one, though.*

'Get ready,' said the rider. 'I'm coming in.'

Hunter watched as the d-bot glided into place. *She's pretty good at flying,* he thought. *I just hope her plan works.*

'I'm lifting the neck up now,' the rider said. 'Let's do it on the count of three.'

Hunter's feet almost touched the neck of the girl's d-bot. He looked down and his tummy flipped.

What if I miss? he thought. *But no – don't think, Hunter.* **Just do it.**

He placed a foot on either side of the d-bot's neck.

'One, two...'

Hunter took a deep breath and
tickled the claw.

'Three!'

The claw opened. Hunter let
go of the dinosaur's leg and
dropped.

Chapter Three

Hunter landed hard on the
d-bot and slid down its neck.
He wrapped his legs and arms
around it. Then he pressed his
face against the metal.

The metal felt cool and hard.
Hunter thought it was the best
feeling ever. *I'm safe,* he
thought.

'Welcome aboard,' the rider
yelled above the wind. 'I'm
Charlie. Are you okay?'

'Yep,' Hunter said, sitting up tall.
'Er…thanks for getting me.'

'Sure, no problem,' Charlie said.
'Now we need to get your d-bot
back.'

As they flew out from under the
dinosaur, there was a loud
noise.

Snap! Snap! Snap! Snap!

'Oh, no! Go faster,' Hunter cried. 'That jaw is toothless, but strong and deep. If it bites your d-bot's tail, it won't let go.'

Snap! Snap! Snap! Snap!

'Don't worry,' Charlie said. 'Our tail has a solid metal ball on the end. It will be sorry if it bites us. And I can shoot the ball at the push of a button.'

Like a cannonball – **cool!**
thought Hunter. *I wonder what
else she's thought of.*

'But you're right,' Charlie said.
'We need to get going. Hang on
tight. I'm turning up the speed.
I want it to keep chasing us,
though.'

'Yes, we need to make it land,' Hunter said. 'Gently! We don't want my d-bot hurt.'

'I'll land on that little beach up ahead,' Charlie said. 'This dinosaur needs to land on its feet. I'm hoping it will drop your d-bot in the water first.'

That's what I was thinking,
thought Hunter. *Weird.*

The d-bot sped towards the
island with the Q chasing it.

'Squuuaaaark!
Squuuaaaark!
Squuuaaaark!
Squuuaaaark!'

'It sounds hungry,' Charlie yelled above the cries.

'Yes,' agreed Hunter. 'And it wants us for lunch! Qs ate other dinosaurs.'

'No, they ate fish,' Charlie said. 'Still, there were no humans when they ruled the sky. We can't know for sure if we're safe.'

'I think—' Hunter began.

'Shhh,' Charlie said. 'I need to think of a plan. I can't think while someone else is talking.'

Fine with me, bossy boots, thought Hunter. *I hate noise and chatter too.*

Charlie pointed the d-bot's nose down. She was deep in thought. So was Hunter.

I've got it,' Charlie said, getting ready to land. 'My d-bot is taller than this Q. The Q won't like that. Also, we can take off from a standing pose. The Q can't. So we...'

'...should corner it,' they both said at the same time.

Charlie landed her d-bot smoothly on the beach. Then she ran it towards a cliff wall. As it reached the wall, they heard a noise. **Splash!**

'Sounds like a soft landing for my d-bot,' Hunter said.

Thump! Thump!

'And that's our Q landing on the sand,' Charlie added.

Charlie turned her d-bot around so that it was facing the dinosaur.

'Now to put the rest of my plan into action,' she said.

Chapter Four

The Q lowered its wings to
stand on all fours. It stared
hungrily at Charlie and Hunter.
They were trapped by the cliff
walls. Or so it thought.

'Time to stand my d-bot up,'
Charlie said. 'Quick, sit behind
me and hang on!'

Hunter didn't want to sit
behind Charlie. He wanted to
drive her d-bot.

'Hurry,' Charlie said. 'We don't
have much time!' Hunter slid to
the ground.

Just then, the dinosaur charged
at them. 'Oh no! Jump on the
tail,' Charlie cried as her d-bot
stood up then left the ground.

As the net fell over the dinosaur, it struggled to get free.

'Be still,' Hunter said. 'Soon you'll be back where you belong.'

Charlie hit the teleport button on her d-band. 'We did it,' she called.

Then she landed her d-bot on the sand near Hunter.

The dinosaur began to vanish.
'Teleporting is so cool,' Charlie
said.

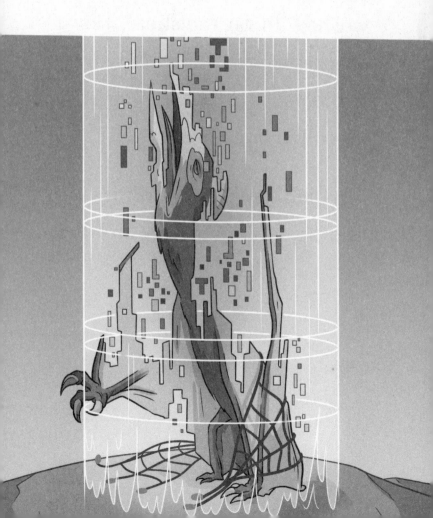

Hunter ran to his d-bot. It had washed up on the shore. He checked it over. 'Nothing else is broken besides the remote,' he called back to Charlie.

'I'm glad my plan worked,' Charlie said, gathering up the net.

It was my plan too, thought Hunter. *I just didn't get to say it. It's weird how we thought the same things.* Hunter frowned. *And more than once.*

Just then, Hunter and Charlie's d-bands flashed. It was Ms Stegg. 'Good job, team!' she said.

Hunter looked at Charlie. *She had to save me*, he thought. *Now she'll tell Ms Stegg all about it.*

'Thanks,' Charlie said into her d-band's speaker. 'Hunter was great. I don't think I could have done it alone.'

Hunter blinked, then looked away.

'The dinosaur is safely back in the park now,' Ms Stegg replied. 'Time to return to base. See you both shortly. Over and out.'

'Are you ready to teleport?' Charlie asked.

'Er...maybe,' Hunter mumbled. He hadn't known *they* could teleport like the dinos.

Hunter had left the base so fast, he hadn't asked about coming back. *I wonder what else I don't know*, he thought. *Now I'm going to have to ask her how to teleport.* His cheeks burned.

'Teleporting feels a bit weird the first time,' Charlie said.

Hunter looked at her. 'Weird how?'

'Things get all misty, and what you can see fades to nothing,' she said. 'Then the mist clears, and you're inside the base. It's super-quick. Oh, and you'll feel a bit cold. Should we do it together?'

Hunter shrugged. 'Why not?'

'Lean against your d-bot,' Charlie said. 'You need to be touching it for it to come with you. Now, press the talk and teleport buttons on your d-band at once. On the count of three. **One, two, three...**'

They hit the buttons at exactly the same time.

Chapter Five

Hunter, Charlie and their d-bots
were standing at D-Bot Squad
base. 'This is the launch pad
that I left from,' Hunter said.
'You're right, Charlie, teleporting
is cool.'

'Welcome back,' Ms Stegg said.
'Follow me, please.'

Hunter and Charlie followed
Ms Stegg into the control room.
Lights were flashing from every
screen. Hunter gaped at them.
'What's going on? Are they
what I think they are?'

'All these dots are dinosaurs on
the loose,' Ms Stegg said. 'The
flashes are the D-Bot Squad
teams chasing them.'

Hunter frowned at the screens.
Seven flashes – there must be
lots more of us, he thought.
And I thought I was special. Ha!

'Is everything okay, Hunter?'
Ms Stegg asked.

'Everything's fine,' Hunter said,
a little too quickly.

Then Hunter pointed to the screen. 'Which of those dots am I going after next?'

Ms Stegg pointed. 'That's the dinosaur that you both need to catch next. It's very big and heavy. **It won't be easy.**'

Hunter had to stop himself from groaning out loud. Charlie was cool. But he didn't want a partner. He wanted to catch dinosaurs all by himself.

Ms Stegg looked at Hunter. 'You must work as a team.'

'What kind of dino is it?' asked Charlie.

'A stegosaurus,' answered Ms Stegg.

Hunter's mind whirred.

'You'll have to change your d-bots,' said Ms Stegg. 'Work quickly. This dinosaur is eating and stomping its way through our forests. I'll send its location to your d-bands while you work. You can teleport straight there when you're ready.'

Hunter and Charlie moved in front of the build-a-bot screens.

I need to get through thick forest, Hunter thought, *and move fast. What else? Ah! A new remote.*

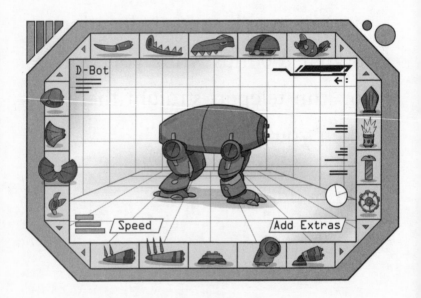

'Done,' said Hunter, pressing the
parts button.

The parts began popping out
from a machine on the far wall.
Hunter grabbed them. He
started building, using the tools
on his tool belt.

When he was finished, Hunter
looked over at Charlie. She was
still building.

Hunter thought about the steg eating up the forest. *This dino isn't smart, and it's super-slow,* he thought. *I can deal with it. I'll get a head start.*

Hunter leapt onto his d-bot. He hit the teleport button on his d-band.

And then he was gone. He didn't wait for Charlie.

Chapter Six

Hunter was now in thick forest.

It's so hot and steamy here, he thought. He looked around and listened. *The steg must be here somewhere.*

I need to clear a path but not hurt the forest, thought Hunter.

He pushed a button. The frills of his d-bot's neck started to move. As they whirred around, they parted the ferns and trees.

Hunter came to a flattened path. His d-band flashed. It was Charlie. 'Where are you, and why didn't you wait for me?'

'You weren't ready,' Hunter said. 'I'm in the forest. I've found the steg's tracks. It's left a wide path where it's been.'

'Don't go after it alone,' Charlie said. 'Wait. I'll be there soon!'

But Hunter didn't wait. He followed the path to a waterfall. And there was the steg!

Hunter climbed down from his d-bot. He crept up behind the steg. *You're awesome,* he thought. *But you'd eat a forest in two days! Maybe that's why you died out.*

Braaapt-phrrrr-pppfft!

Hunter giggled. **'Gross!** You did a fart!' Then he remembered something he'd read.

Stegs made never-ending gas, from all the plants they ate, he thought. *They were one big walking, smelly fart! I need to move away.*

But before Hunter could move, the dinosaur let out a huge cloud of gas.

Braaapt-phrrrr-pppfft-plop!

Hunter was swallowed up by a fog of stinkiness. It was so stinky, he fell to the ground, dizzy.

Then the steg turned its head towards Hunter...

And everything went black.

Will Hunter survive

the giant fart?

Read Book 4, *Big Stink*,

to find out...

Join
D-BOT SQUAD
Catch all 8 books!